Hairy Maclary and Zachary Quack

Lynley Dodd

Gareth Stevens Publishing
A WORLD ALMANAC EDUCATION GROUP COMPANY

It was drowsily warm,
with dozens of bees
lazily buzzing
through flowers and trees.
Hairy Maclary decided to choose
a space in the shade
for his afternoon
snooze.
He dozily dreamed
as he lay on his back
when …

3

pittery pattery,
skittery scattery,
Z I P
round the corner
came
Zachary Quack,

who wanted to frolic
and footle
and play
but ...

Hairy Maclary
skedaddled
away.

Over the lawn
and asparagus bed
went Hairy Maclary
to hide in the shed.
He lurked in the shadows
all dusty and black
but …

pittery pattery,
skittery scattery,
Z I P
round the corner
came
Zachary Quack.

Out of the garden
and into the trees
jumped Hairy Maclary
with springs
in his knees.
He hid in the grass
at the side of the track
but ...

pittery pattery,
skittery scattery,
Z I P
round the corner
came
Zachary Quack.

Down to the river
through willow and reed
raced Hairy Maclary
at double the speed.
Into the water
he flew with a
S M A C K
but …

pittery pattery,
skittery scattery,
Z I P
round the corner
came
Zachary Quack,
who dizzily dived
in the craziest way,
whirling
and swirling
in showers of spray.

Hairy Maclary
was off in a flash,
a flurry of bubbles,
a dog paddle splash.
He swam to the side
and floundered about,
he tried
and he tried
but he C O U L D N ' T
climb out.
Scrabbling upward
and slithering back ...
when

pittery pattery,
skittery scattery,
Z I P
through the water
came
Zachary Quack,
who sped round a corner
and,
showing the way,
led Hairy Maclary
up, up
and away.

Then,
soggy and shivering,
back up the track
went Hairy Maclary
with
Zachary Quack.

It was drowsily warm,
with dozens of bees
lazily buzzing
through flowers
and trees.
Hairy Maclary
decided to choose
a place in the shade
for his afternoon
snooze.
He dozily dreamed
as he lay on his back …

tucked up together
with
Zachary Quack.

For a free color catalog describing Gareth Stevens' list of high-quality books and multimedia programs, call 1-800-542-2595 (USA) or 1-800-461-9120 (Canada). Gareth Stevens Publishing's Fax: (414) 225-0377.

Other GOLD STAR FIRST READER Millennium Editions:

A Dragon in a Wagon
Hairy Maclary from Donaldson's Dairy
Hairy Maclary Scattercat
Hairy Maclary's Caterwaul Caper
Hairy Maclary's Rumpus at the Vet
The Smallest Turtle
SNIFF-SNUFF-SNAP!

and also by Lynley Dodd:

Hairy Maclary, Sit
Hairy Maclary's Showbusiness
The Minister's Cat ABC
Schnitzel von Krumm Forget-Me-Not
Slinky Malinki Catflaps

Library of Congress Cataloging-in-Publication Data

Dodd, Lynley.
    Hairy Maclary and Zachary Quack / by Lynley Dodd.
       p. cm. — (Gold star first readers)
    Summary: A small and very determined duckling sets out to play
with a rather reluctant dog.
      ISBN 0-8368-2676-0 (lib. bdg.)
      [1. Dogs—Fiction. 2. Ducks—Fiction. 3. Stories in rhyme.] I. Title.
II. Series.
    PZ8.3.D637Had   2000
    [E]—dc21   00-029170

This edition first published in 2000 by
Gareth Stevens Publishing
A World Almanac Education Group Company
1555 North RiverCenter Drive, Suite 201
Milwaukee, WI 53212 USA

First published in 1999 in New Zealand by Mallinson Rendel Publishers Ltd. Original © 1999 by Lynley Dodd.

Printed in the United States of America

1 2 3 4 5 6 7 8 9 04 03 02 01 00